First edition published by Blended Mix Publishing
Contact: www.blendedmixpublishing.com

Cover Illustration by Shehan Arts
Manuscript Illustrations by Lily Walther
Author Photo by Wanda Reyes
Cover Layout and Formatting by Meg Delagrange-Belfon

PRINTED IN THE UNITED STATES OF AMERICA

Illustrated by Lilly Walther

Valentino's Purpose

Author Wanda Reyes

This book belongs to:

Dedication

I would like to begin this book by expressing my heartfelt gratitude and admiration for Valentino, the remarkable goldendoodle who has not only touched my life but the lives of others. He has also served as the inspiration behind this enchanting story. It is with great privilege and joy that I dedicate this book to Valentino, whose boundless love and unwavering loyalty have forever captured my heart.

In addition to Valentino, I extend my dedication to all the extraordinary individuals who have shared their love and affection for him throughout his incredible journey.

To Michael Torres and Danni Carmine
for your creative input and technical expertise
in the completion of this labor of love.

Scan the Code to Watch
Valentino's Special Message

Introduction

Through engaging storytelling and delightful illustrations, "Valentino's Purpose" celebrates the beauty of diversity, the power of self-expression, and the importance of accepting others for who they are. This uplifting tale not only entertains but also encourages young readers to stand tall, express themselves boldly, and radiate love and acceptance to the world around them.

So, get ready to embark on a fashion-filled journey with Valentino, where you'll discover that being different is what makes us all so special. Together, let's embrace our true selves, celebrate our unique styles, and learn that love and acceptance are the most fashionable accessories of all!

Hello, friend!

From day one, Mom has always
said that I was sent from heaven.
From then on, I knew I was destined
for greatness, and God knew that too.
He put me into the life of someone who
needed me, and He knew I would give
her unconditional love, just like the love
He gives to me. Knowing that
I would be brave and strong,
Mom named me Valentino!

As soon as I was able
to walk properly, she
started teaching me
all sorts of new things!
I even learned to smile
for the camera!

When I was old enough, Mom said, "Valentino, you are going to school to be a service dog!" I was so excited to make new friends and learn all about being a service animal. So back-to-school shopping we went.

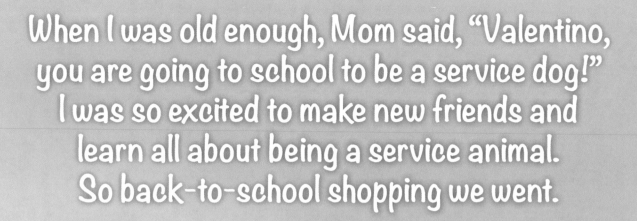

Mom bought me new clothes, shoes, and a backpack that she filled with all my favorite treats! The first day of school couldn't come fast enough!

They laughed and made fun of me because I was wearing shoes and a shirt. I felt very sad.

When I hopped on the bus after school that day, I was surrounded by all the other dogs in my class, who were still making fun of me.

I just wanted to get home and never go back.

school

As soon as I got to my stop, I hopped off the bus and ran as fast as I could to tell my mom what had happened.

With tears running down my face, I said, "Mommy, the other dogs were mean and mocked me for wearing clothes and shoes."

My mom wiped the tears from my face and said, "Don't be sad, my Valentino. It's okay to be different. You are unique, and you are special. You are meant to do great things. I love you so much."

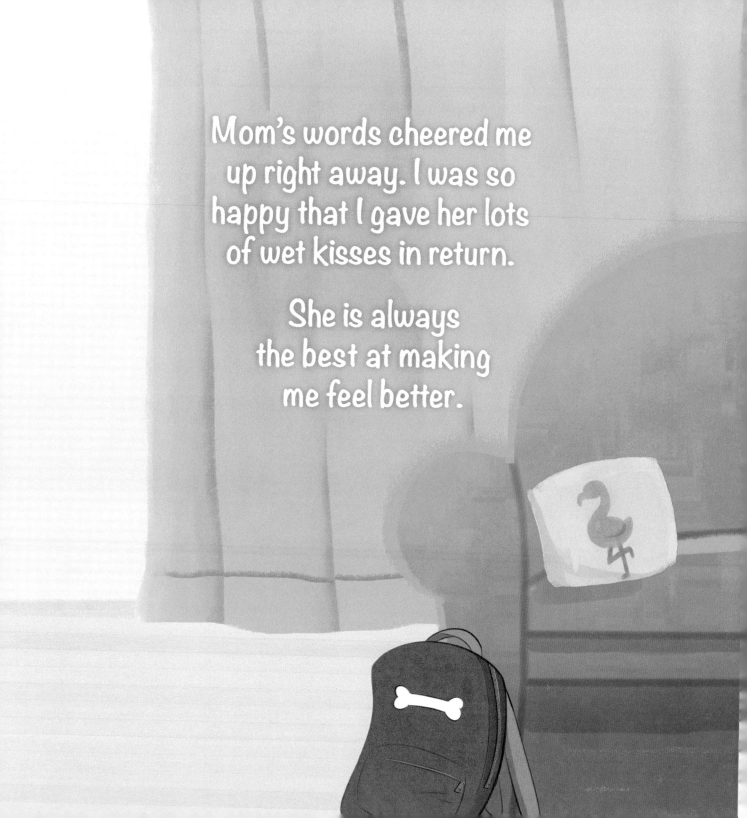

Mom's words cheered me
up right away. I was so
happy that I gave her lots
of wet kisses in return.

She is always
the best at making
me feel better.

The next morning, I got ready for school and decided to wear my cool light-up shoes with my matching red shirt. This time, I would go in with positivity and confidence because I remembered what Mom said about being different.

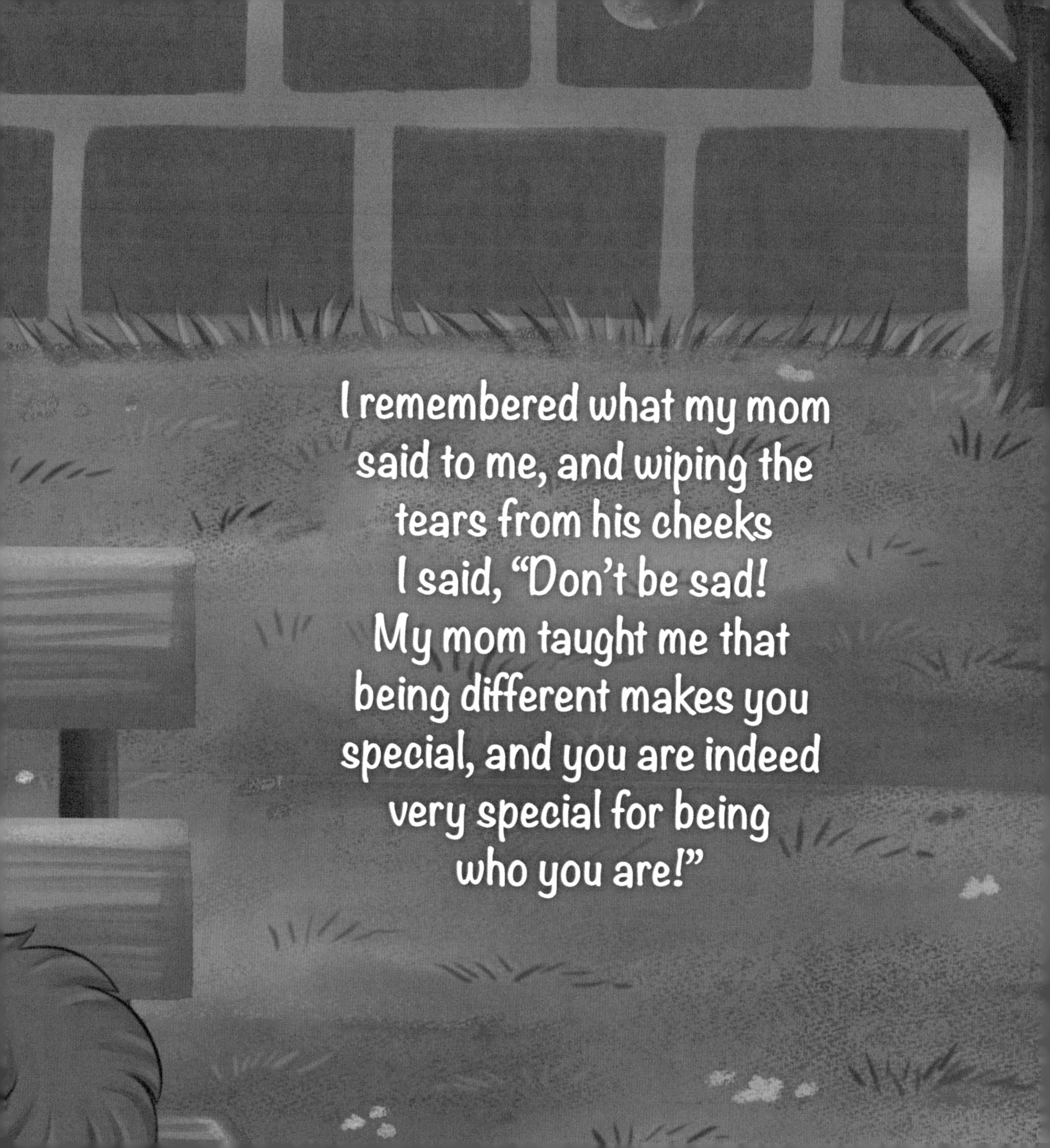

I remembered what my mom
said to me, and wiping the
tears from his cheeks
I said, "Don't be sad!
My mom taught me that
being different makes you
special, and you are indeed
very special for being
who you are!"

The classmate wiped the last of his tears. "My name is Buddy, and you are right! Being different is special. Thank you!" he said, gleefully.

"You are welcome! I'm Valentino, and you have me as a friend from now on."

The next day, Buddy pulled Valentino in his favorite red wagon. They both smiled and sang on their way to school. Valentino wore his red hoodie, matching shoes, and a vibrant smile.

This time, Buddy was proud of his long blue hair and wore a cool baseball cap.

Valentino and Buddy had so much fun together at school now that they could be themselves.

As the school year continued, they even made friends with other dogs!

DOG PARK

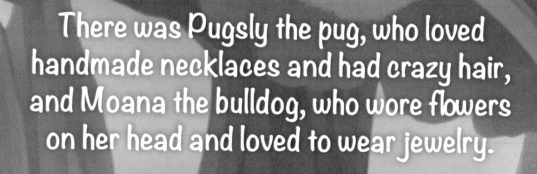

There was Pugsly the pug, who loved
handmade necklaces and had crazy hair,
and Moana the bulldog, who wore flowers
on her head and loved to wear jewelry.

No matter what they wore or
how they looked, they were all
special in their unique ways.

At the end of their schooling, Valentino with his many outfits, Buddy with his blue hair, Pugsly with all his necklaces, and Moana with all her flowers and jewelry, graduated from school with honors. They were on their way to being the best service dogs ever!

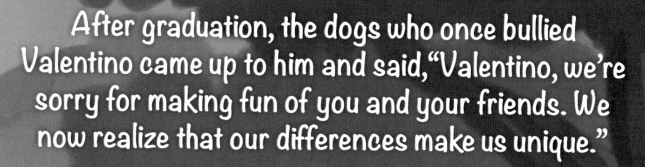

After graduation, the dogs who once bullied Valentino came up to him and said, "Valentino, we're sorry for making fun of you and your friends. We now realize that our differences make us unique."

Valentino gave them an enchanting smile and replied, "It's okay! I forgive you!" He thought for a moment, then added, "Do you want to hang out with us?"

And so, the dogs who once laughed at Valentino's differences joined his group of unique individuals, and they all became great friends. Each friend brought their uniqueness to the group and accepted their differences, no matter what they were.

"In order to be irreplaceable, one must always be different."

COCO CHANEL

Meet the Author

WANDA REYES, a California-born writer, is a passionate advocate for the love and well-being of animals. Her upcoming book, inspired by her precious Goldendoodle Valentino, beautifully captures her deep affection for animals and her desire to make a positive impact on all readers.

As an artist, mother, grandmother, and great-grandmother, Wanda's life has been a rich tapestry of experiences that have taught her the importance of faith, love, belonging, and celebrating uniqueness. It is through these lessons that she has penned her latest work, which aims to touch the lives of all young and adult readers, especially those who have been touched by differences.

Wanda's book is a heartwarming tale that not only showcases the special bond between humans and their furry friends but also celebrates the beauty of diversity and the value of acceptance. Through relatable characters and a story filled with warmth and hope, Wanda hopes to inspire all readers to embrace their own uniqueness and foster empathy towards others.

CONNECT WITH *Wanda*

 DTAILSBYVALENTINO@GMAIL.COM

 WWW.DTAILSBYVALENTINO.COM

CONNECT WITH *Lilly*

 WALTHERLILLY8@GMAIL.COM

 WALTHERLILLY8.WIXSITE.COM/GALLERY

Valentino

Made in the USA
Middletown, DE
12 May 2024

54235322R00031

Happy 1st Birthday!

Happy Birthday!
Enjoy your special day!

You are turning **one** today,
it's such a special day!

You're going to have a party,
where the kids can play and play.

Your friends will come
to celebrate...

They'll have a lot of fun.

They'll play some games,

and have some cake,

and skip, and jump, and run!

You might have cotton candy...

and you might play on the slide!

Or maybe a nice puppet show,
if you all stay inside!

They'll bring balloons,
and presents...

And there might just be a clown!

And some of your good buddies
will be jumping up and down!

Maybe you will go outside,
and play with all your friends.

The day will be your special day,
from morning till it ends.

So, Happy, Happy Birthday!

To a boy who's really sweet!

A boy that's super-special...

from his head
down to his feet!

Happy 1st Birthday!

Sally was born in Jackson, Michigan. She has lived all over the country with her husband, Fred. They have 3 grown children, and they all live in Louisville, KY. She has written over 30 children's books and had her first book published in 2000. Sneaky Snail Stories are all sweet and simple rhyming books with really cute illustrations. You can see all the Sneaky Snail Stories at: www.sneakysnailstories.com
Other books by Sally:

No Pancakes for Puppy
Grandma and Grandpa Love You
Your Aunt Loves You
The Best Day

Emma's Hilarious Horse Book (personalized for boys or girls with cats, dogs, penguins or frogs)
Emma, the Super, Amazing, Awesome, Intelligent, Girly-Girl (personalized)
Noah the Basketball Star (personalized for several sports for boys or girls)
Noah's Very Own Cook Book (personalized for boys or girls)
Grandma and Grandpa Love Emma (personalized from any relative for boys or girls)
Emma Turns One! (personalized for boys or girls ages 1-6)   and many more....

website: www.sneakysnailstories.com   facebook: Sneaky Snail Stories
Etsy: (search for) thesneakysnailstore   Amazon: (search for) Sally Helmick North

The Best Day!

written and illustrated by Sally Helmick North

No Cookies for Kitty!

written and illustrated by Sally Helmick North

No Pancakes for Puppy!

written and illustrated by Sally Helmick North

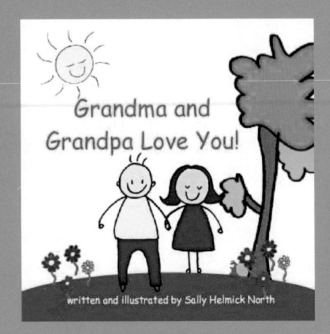

Grandma and Grandpa Love You!

written and illustrated by Sally Helmick North

Made in the USA
Middletown, DE
07 December 2016